Munschworks
The First Munsch Collection

Munschworks
The First Munsch Collection

stories by Robert Munsch
illustrations by Michael Martchenko

Annick Press Ltd.
Toronto • New York • Vancouver

Munschworks ©1998 Annick Press Ltd.

Second printing, May 1999

The Paper Bag Princess
  ©1980 Bob Munsch Enterprises Ltd. (text)
  ©1980 Michael Martchenko (art)
The Fire Station
  ©1991 Bob Munsch Enterprises Ltd. (text)
  ©1983 Michael Martchenko (art)
I Have to Go!
  ©1987 Bob Munsch Enterprises Ltd. (text)
  ©1987 Michael Martchenko (art)
David's Father
  ©1983 Bob Munsch Enterprises Ltd. (text)
  ©1983 Michael Martchenko (art)
Thomas' Snowsuit
  ©1985 Bob Munsch Enterprises Ltd. (text)
  ©1985 Michael Martchenko (art)

We acknowledge the support of the Canada Council
for the Arts for our publishing program.
We also thank the Ontario Arts Council.

Cataloguing in Publication Data

Munsch, Robert N., 1945-
  Munschworks : the first Munsch collection

ISBN 1-55037-523-7

I. Martchenko, Michael. II. Title.

PS8576.U575M86 1998 jC813.'54 C98-930311-X
PZ7.M86Mu 1998

The art in this book was rendered in watercolor.
The text was typeset in Century Oldstyle and Adlib.

Distributed in Canada by: Published in the U.S.A. by Annick Press (U.S.) Ltd.
Firefly Books Ltd. Distributed in the U.S.A. by:
3680 Victoria Park Avenue Firefly Books (U.S.) Inc.
Willowdale, ON P.O. Box 1338
M2H 3K1 Ellicott Station
  Buffalo, NY 14205

Printed and bound in Belgium.

Contents

The Paper Bag Princess

by **Robert Munsch**
illustrated by
Michael Martchenko

Elizabeth was a beautiful princess. She lived in a castle and had expensive princess clothes. She was going to marry a prince named Ronald.

Unfortunately, a dragon smashed her castle, burned all her clothes with his fiery breath, and carried off Prince Ronald.

Elizabeth decided to chase the dragon and get Ronald back.

She looked everywhere for something to wear, but the only thing she could find that was not burnt was a paper bag. So she put on the paper bag and followed the dragon.

He was easy to follow, because he left a trail of burnt forests and horses' bones.

Finally, Elizabeth came to a cave with a large door that had a huge knocker on it. She took hold of the knocker and banged on the door.

The dragon stuck his nose out of the door and said, "Well, a princess! I love to eat princesses, but I have already eaten a whole castle today. I am a very busy dragon. Come back tomorrow."

He slammed the door so fast that Elizabeth almost got her nose caught.

Elizabeth grabbed the knocker and banged on the door again.

The dragon stuck his nose out of the door and said, "Go away. I love to eat princesses, but I have already eaten a whole castle today. I am a very busy dragon. Come back tomorrow."

"Wait," shouted Elizabeth. "Is it true that you are the smartest and fiercest dragon in the whole world?"

"Yes," said the dragon.

"Is it true," said Elizabeth, "that you can burn up ten forests with your fiery breath?"

"Oh, yes," said the dragon, and he took a huge, deep breath and breathed out so much fire that he burnt up fifty forests.

"Fantastic," said Elizabeth, and the dragon took another huge breath and breathed out so much fire that he burnt up one hundred forests.

"Magnificent," said Elizabeth, and the dragon took another huge breath, but this time nothing came out. The dragon didn't even have enough fire left to cook a meatball.

Elizabeth said, "Dragon, is it true that you can fly around the world in just ten seconds?"

"Why, yes," said the dragon, and jumped up and flew all the way around the world in just ten seconds.

He was very tired when he got back, but Elizabeth shouted, "Fantastic, do it again!"

So the dragon jumped up and flew around
the whole world in just twenty seconds.
When he got back he was too tired to talk,
and he lay down and went straight to sleep.

Elizabeth whispered, very softly, "Hey, dragon." The dragon didn't move at all.

She lifted up the dragon's ear and put her head right inside. She shouted as loud as she could, "Hey, dragon!"

The dragon was so tired he didn't even move.

Elizabeth walked right over the dragon and opened the door to the cave.

There was Prince Ronald. He looked at her and said, "Elizabeth, you are a mess! You smell like ashes, your hair is all tangled and you are wearing a dirty old paper bag. Come back when you are dressed like a real princess."

"Ronald," said Elizabeth, "your clothes are really pretty and your hair is very neat. You look like a real prince, but you are a bum."

They didn't get married after all.

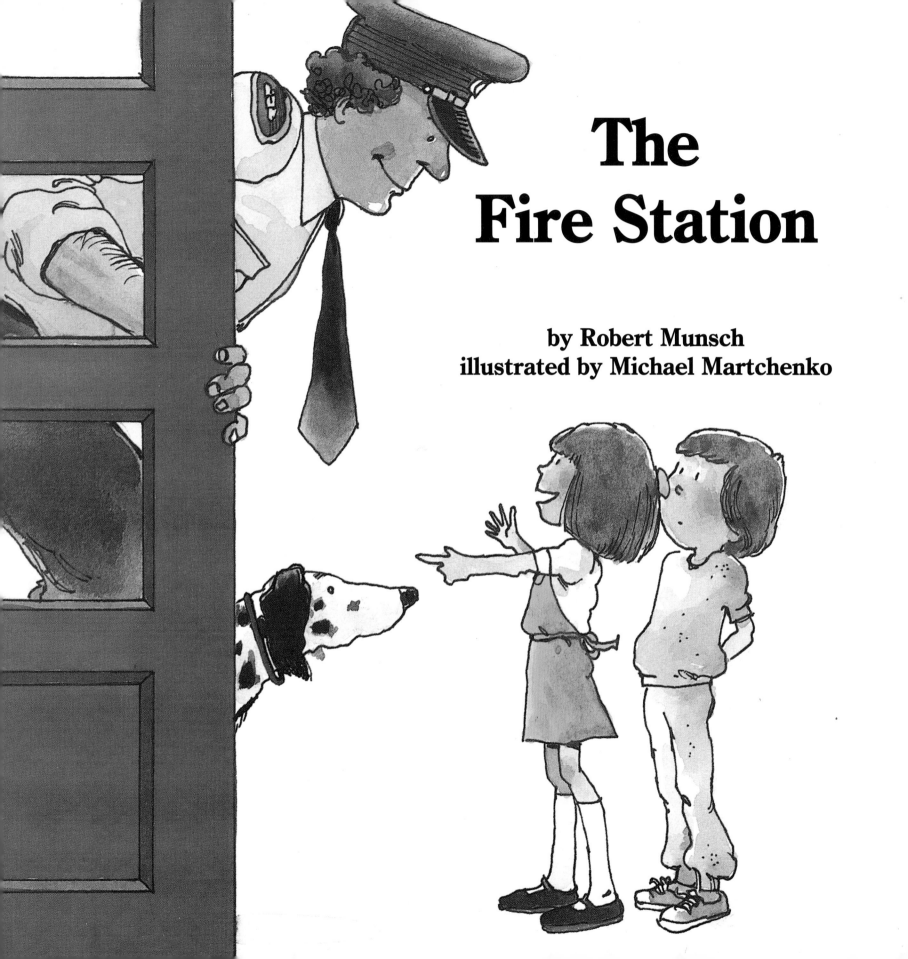

The
Fire Station

by Robert Munsch
illustrated by Michael Martchenko

*M*ichael and Sheila were walking down the street. As they passed the fire station Sheila said, "Michael! Let's go ride a fire truck."

"Well," said Michael, "I think maybe I should ask my mother, and I think maybe I should ask my father and I think maybe…"

"I think we should go in," said Sheila. Then she grabbed Michael's hand and pulled him up to the door.

Sheila knocked: BLAM – BLAM – BLAM – BLAM – BLAM. A large fireman came out and asked, "What can I do for you?"

"Well," said Michael, "maybe you could show us a fire truck and hoses and rubber boots and ladders and all sorts of stuff like that."

"Certainly," said the fireman.

"And maybe," said Sheila, "you will let us drive a fire truck?"

"Certainly not," said the fireman.

They went in and looked at ladders and hoses and big rubber boots. Then they looked at little fire trucks and big fire trucks and enormous fire trucks. When they were done Michael said, "Let's go."

"Right," said Sheila. "Let's go into the enormous fire truck."

While they were in the truck, the fire alarm went off: CLANG – CLANG – CLANG – CLANG – CLANG.

"Oh, no!" said Michael.

"Oh, yes!" said Sheila. Then she grabbed Michael and pulled him into the back seat.

Firemen came running from all over. They slid down poles and ran down stairs. Then they jumped onto the truck and drove off. The firemen didn't look in the back seat. Michael and Sheila were in the back seat.

They came to an enormous fire. Lots of yucky-colored smoke got all over everything. It colored Michael yellow, green and blue. It colored Sheila purple, green and yellow.

When the fire chief saw them he said, "What are you doing here!"

Sheila said, "We came in the fire truck. We thought maybe it was a bus. We thought maybe it was a taxi. We thought maybe it was an elevator. We thought maybe..."

"I think maybe I'd better take you home," said the fire chief. He put Michael and Sheila in his car and drove them away.

When Michael got home he knocked on the door. His mother opened it and said, "You messy boy! You can't come in and play with Michael! You're too dirty." She slammed the door right in Michael's face.

"My own mother," said Michael. "She didn't even know me." He knocked on the door again.

His mother opened the door and said, "You dirty boy! You can't come in and play with Michael. You're too dirty. You're absolutely filthy. You're a total mess. You're...Oh, my!...Oh, no!...YOU'RE MICHAEL!"

Michael went inside and lived in the bathtub for three days until he got clean.

When Sheila came home she knocked on the door. Her father opened it and saw an incredibly messy girl. He said, "You can't come in to play with Sheila. You're too dirty." He slammed the door right in her face.

"Ow," said Sheila. "My own father and he didn't even know me."

She kicked and pounded on the door as loudly as she could. Her father opened the door and said, "Now stop that racket, you dirty girl. You can't come in to play with Sheila. You're too dirty. You're absolutely filthy. You're a total mess. You're...Oh, my!...Oh, no!... YOU'RE SHEILA!"

"Right," said Sheila, "I went to a fire in the back of a fire truck and I got all smoky. I WASN'T EVEN SCARED."

Sheila went inside and lived in the bathtub for five days until she got clean.

Then Michael took Sheila on a walk past the police station. He told her, "If you ever take me in another fire truck, I am going to ask the police to put you in jail."

"JAIL!" yelled Sheila. "Let's go look at the jail! What a great idea!"

"Oh, no!" yelled Michael, and Sheila grabbed his hand and pulled him into the police station.

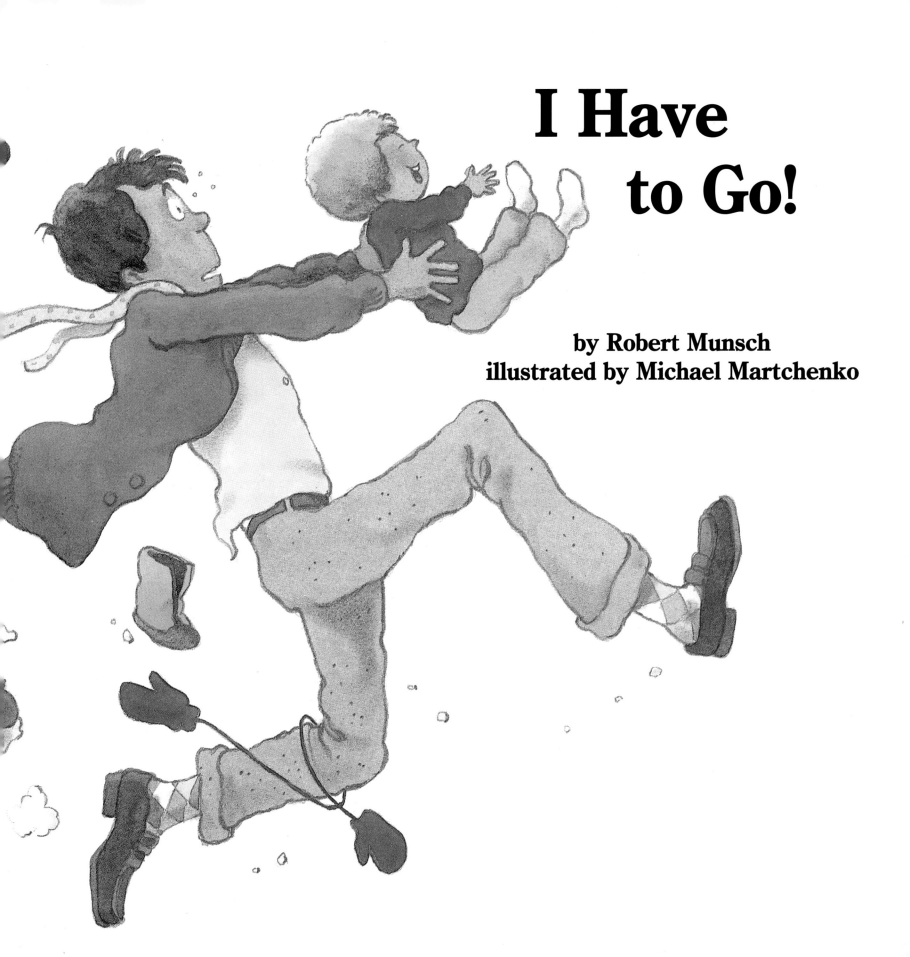

I Have
to Go!

by Robert Munsch
illustrated by Michael Martchenko

*O*ne day Andrew's mother and father were taking him to see his grandma and grandpa. Before they put him in the car his mother said, "Andrew, do you have to go pee?"

Andrew said, "No, no, no, no, no."

His father said, very slowly and clearly, "Andrew, do you have to go pee?"

"No, no, no, no," said Andrew. "I have decided never to go pee again."

So they put Andrew into the car, fastened his seatbelt and gave him lots of books, and lots of toys, and lots of crayons, and drove off down the road—VAROOMMM. They had been driving for just one minute when Andrew yelled, "I HAVE TO GO PEE!"

"YIKES," said the father.

"OH NO," said the mother.

Then the father said, "Now, Andrew, wait just five minutes. In five minutes we will come to a gas station where you can go pee."

Andrew said, "I have to go pee RIGHT NOW!"

So the mother stopped the car— SCREEEEECH. Andrew jumped out of the car and peed behind a bush.

When they got to Grandma's and Grandpa's house, Andrew wanted to go out to play. It was snowing, and he needed a snowsuit. Before they put on the snowsuit, the mother and the father and the grandma and the grandpa all said, "ANDREW! DO YOU HAVE TO GO PEE?"

Andrew said, "No, no, no, no, no."

So they put on Andrew's snowsuit. It had five zippers, 10 buckles and 17 snaps. It took them half an hour to get the snowsuit on.

Andrew walked out into the back yard, threw one snowball and yelled, "I HAVE TO GO PEE."

The father and the mother and the grandma and the grandpa all ran outside, got Andrew out of the snowsuit and carried him to the bathroom.

When Andrew came back down they had a
nice long dinner. Then it was time for Andrew
to go to bed.

Before they put Andrew into bed, the mother
and the father and the grandma and the
grandpa all said, "ANDREW! DO YOU HAVE
TO GO PEE?"

Andrew said, "No, no, no, no, no."

So his mother gave him a kiss, and his father gave him a kiss, and his grandma gave him a kiss, and his grandpa gave him a kiss.

"Just wait," said the mother, "he's going to yell and say he has to go pee."

"Oh," said the father, "he does it every night. It's driving me crazy."

The grandmother said, "I never had these problems with my children."

They waited for five minutes, 10 minutes, 15 minutes, 20 minutes.

The father said, "I think he is asleep."

The mother said, "Yes, I think he is asleep."

The grandmother said, "He is definitely asleep and he didn't yell and say he had to go pee."

Then Andrew said, "I wet my bed."

So the mother and the father and the grandma and the grandpa all changed Andrew's bed and Andrew's pajamas. Then the mother gave him a kiss, and the father gave him a kiss, and the grandma gave him a kiss, and the grandpa gave him a kiss, and the grownups all went downstairs.

They waited five minutes, 10 minutes, 15 minutes, 20 minutes, and from upstairs Andrew yelled, "GRANDPA, DO YOU HAVE TO GO PEE?"

And Grandpa said, "Why, yes, I think I do."

Andrew said, "Well, so do I."

So they both went to the bathroom and peed in the toilet, and Andrew did not wet his bed again that night, not even once.

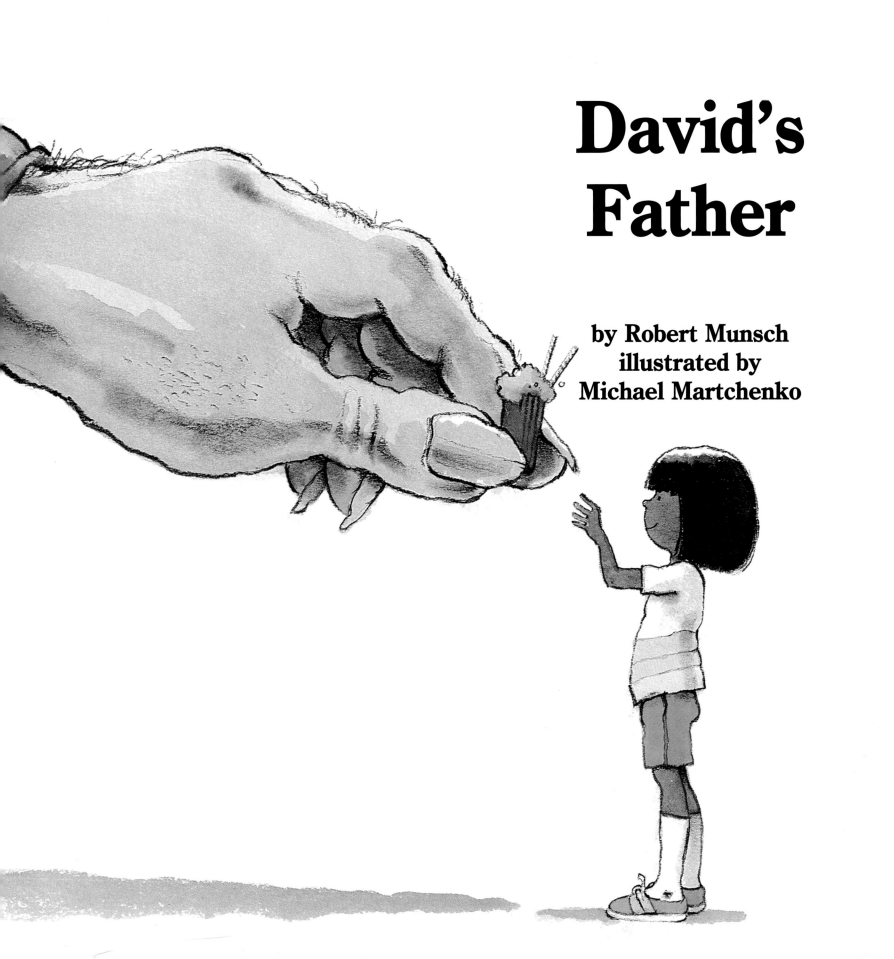

David's Father

by Robert Munsch
illustrated by
Michael Martchenko

*J*ulie was skipping home from school. She came to a large moving van. A man came out carrying a spoon—only it was as big as a shovel. Another man came out carrying a fork—only it was as big as a pitchfork. A third man came out carrying a knife—only it was as big as a flagpole.

"Yikes," said Julie, "I don't want to get to know these people at all."

She ran all the way home and hid under her bed till dinner time.

The next day Julie was skipping home from school again. A boy was standing where the moving van had been. He said, "Hi, my name's David. Would you like to come and play?" Julie looked at him very carefully. He seemed to be a regular sort of boy, so she stayed to play.

At five o'clock, from far away down the street, someone called, "Julie, come and eat."

"That's my mother," said Julie. Then someone called, ***"DAVID!!!"***

"That's my father," said David.

Julie jumped up in the air, ran around in a circle three times, ran home and locked herself in her room till it was time for breakfast the next morning.

The next day Julie was skipping home and she saw David again. He said, "Hi, Julie, do you want to come and play?" Julie looked at him very, very carefully. He seemed to be a regular boy, so she stayed and played.

When it was almost five o'clock, David said, "Julie, please stay for dinner."

But Julie remembered the big knife, the big fork and the big spoon. "Well, I don't know," she said, "maybe it's a bad idea. I think maybe no. Good-bye, good-bye, good-bye."

"Well," said David, "we're having cheese-burgers, chocolate milk shakes and a salad."

"Oh?" said Julie, "I love cheeseburgers. I'll stay, I'll stay."

So they went into the kitchen. There was a small table with cheeseburgers, milk shakes and salads. On the other side of the room there was an enormous table. On it were a spoon as big as a shovel, a fork as big as a pitchfork and a knife as big as a flagpole. "David," whispered Julie, "who sits there?"

"Oh," said David. "That's where my father sits. You can hear him coming now." David's father sounded like this:

broum broum broum

He opened the door.

David's father was a giant. On his table
there were 26 snails, three fried octopuses
and 16 bricks covered with chocolate sauce.

David and Julie ate their cheeseburgers and the father ate the snails. David and Julie drank their milk shakes and the father ate the fried octopuses. David and Julie ate their salads and the father ate his chocolate-covered bricks.

David's father asked Julie if she would like a snail. Julie said no. David's father asked Julie if she would like an octopus. Julie said no. David's father asked Julie if she would like a delicious chocolate-covered brick. Julie said, "No, but please, may I have another milk shake?" So David's father made her another milk shake.

When they were done Julie said, very softly so the father couldn't hear, "David, you don't look very much like your father."

"Well, I'm adopted," said David.

"Oh," said Julie. "Well, do you like your father?"

"He's great," said David, "come for a walk and see."

So they walked down the street. Julie and David skipped, and the father went

broum broum broum.

They came to a road and they couldn't get across. The cars would not stop for David. The cars would not stop for Julie. The father walked into the middle of the road, looked at the cars and yelled,

"stop."

The cars all jumped up into the air, ran around in a circle three times and went back up the street so fast they forgot their tires.

Julie and David crossed the street and went into a store. The man who ran the store didn't like serving kids. They waited five minutes, 10 minutes, 15 minutes. Then David's father came in. He looked at the storekeeper and said, ***"THESE KIDS ARE MY FRIENDS!"*** The man jumped up into the air, ran around the store three times and gave David and Julie three boxes of ice cream, 11 bags of potato chips and 19 life savers, all for free. Julie and David walked down the street and went around a bend.

There were six big kids from grade eight standing in the middle of the sidewalk. They looked at David. They looked at Julie and they looked at the food. Then one big kid reached down and grabbed a box of ice cream. David's father came round the bend. He looked at the big kids and yelled,

"beat it."

They jumped right out of their shirts. They jumped right out of their pants and ran down the street in their underwear. Julie ran after them, but she slipped and scraped her elbow.

David's father picked her up and held her.
Then he put a special giant bandage on her elbow.
Julie said, "Well, David, you do have a very
nice father after all, but he is still kind of scary."

"You think he is scary?" said David.
"Wait till you meet my grandmother."

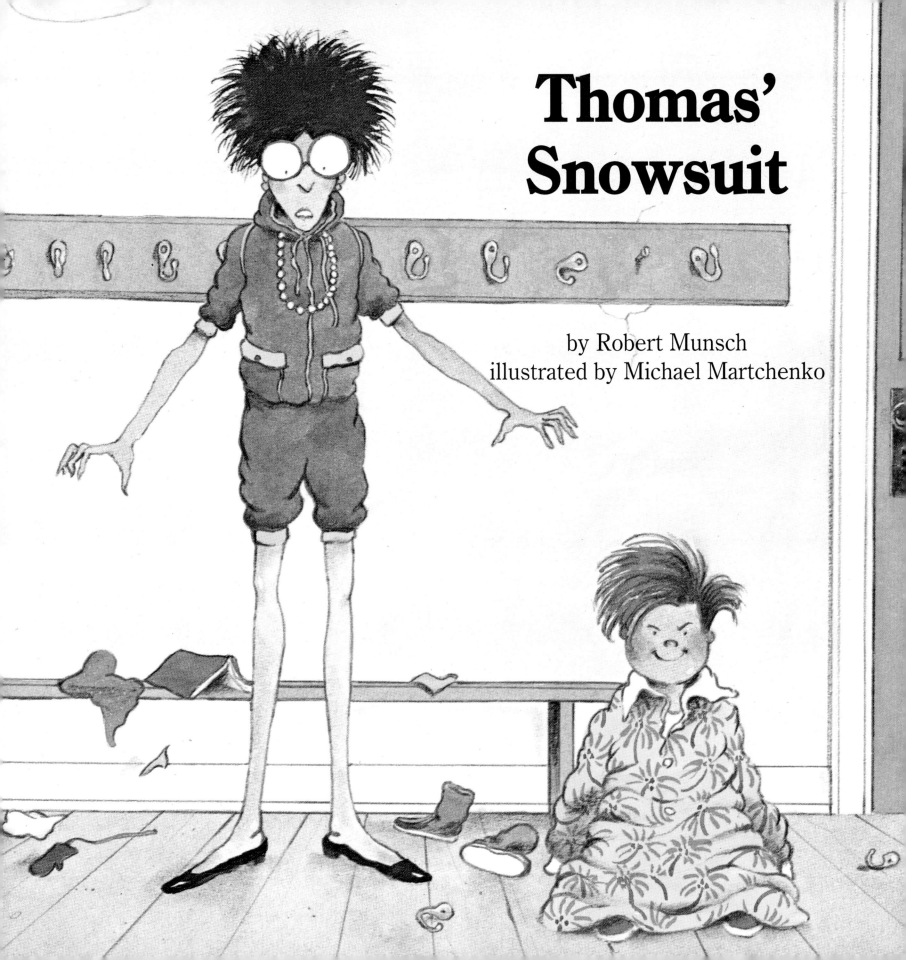

Thomas'
Snowsuit

by Robert Munsch
illustrated by Michael Martchenko

*O*ne day, Thomas' mother bought him a nice new brown snowsuit. When Thomas saw that snowsuit he said, "That is the ugliest thing I have ever seen in my life. If you think that I am going to wear that ugly snowsuit, you are crazy!"

Thomas' mother said, "We will see about that."

The next day, when it was time to go to school, the mother said, "Thomas, please put on your snowsuit," and Thomas said, "NNNNNO."

His mother jumped up and down and said, "Thomas, put on that snowsuit!"

And Thomas said, "NNNNNO!"

So Thomas' mother picked up Thomas in one hand, picked up the snowsuit in the other hand, and she tried to stick them together. They had an enormous fight, and when it was done Thomas was in his snowsuit.

Thomas went off to school and hung up his snowsuit. When it was time to go outside, all the other kids jumped into their snowsuits and ran out the door. But not Thomas.

The teacher looked at Thomas and said, "Thomas, please put on your snowsuit."

Thomas said, "NNNNNO."

The teacher jumped up and down and said, "Thomas, put on that snowsuit."

And Thomas said, "NNNNNO."

So the teacher picked up Thomas in one hand, picked up the snowsuit in the other hand and she tried to stick them together. They had an enormous fight, and when they were done the teacher was wearing Thomas' snowsuit and Thomas was wearing the teacher's dress.

When the teacher saw what she was wearing, she picked up Thomas in one hand and tried to get him back into his snowsuit. They had an enormous fight. When they were done, the snowsuit and the dress were tied into a great big knot on the floor and Thomas and the teacher were in their underclothes.

Just then the door opened, and in walked the principal. The teacher said, "It's Thomas. He won't put on his snowsuit."

The principal gave his very best
PRINCIPAL LOOK and said, "Thomas, put on
your snowsuit."
And Thomas said, "NNNNNO."

So the principal picked up Thomas in one hand and he picked up the teacher in the other hand, and he tried to get them back into their clothes. When he was done, the principal was wearing the teacher's dress, the teacher was wearing the principal's suit and Thomas was still in his underwear.

Then from far out in the playground someone yelled, "Thomas, come and play!" Thomas ran across the room, jumped into his snowsuit, got his boots on in two seconds and ran out the door.

The principal looked at the teacher and said, "Hey, you have on my suit. Take it off right now."

The teacher said, "Oh, no. You have on my dress. You take off my dress first."

Well, they argued and argued and argued, but neither one wanted to change first.

Finally, Thomas came in from recess. He looked at the principal and he looked at the teacher. Thomas picked up the principal in one hand. He picked up the teacher in the other hand. They had an enormous fight and Thomas got everybody back into their clothes.

The next day the principal quit his job and
moved to Arizona, where nobody ever wears a
snowsuit.

The Munsch for Kids series:

The Dark
Mud Puddle
The Paper Bag Princess
The Boy in the Drawer
Jonathan Cleaned Up, Then He Heard a Sound
Murmel Murmel Murmel
Millicent and the Wind
Mortimer
The Fire Station
Angela's Airplane
David's Father
Thomas' Snowsuit
50 Below Zero
I Have to Go!
Moira's Birthday
A Promise is a Promise
Pigs
Something Good
Show and Tell
Purple, Green and Yellow
Wait and See
Where is Gah-Ning?
From Far Away
Stephanie's Ponytail
Munschworks 2

Many Munsch titles are available in French and/or
Spanish. Please contact your favorite supplier.